I Love
Christmas

For Nanny and Pa Wilson

SIMON & SCHUSTER BOOKS FOR YOUNG READERS
An imprint of Simon & Schuster Children's Publishing Division
1230 Avenue of the Americas, New York, New York 10020
Text and illustrations copyright © 2009 by Anna Walker
First published by Scholastic Australia Pty Limited in 2009
This edition published under license from Scholastic Australia Pty Limited
First U.S. edition 2009
All rights reserved, including the right of reproduction in whole
or in part in any form.
SIMON & SCHUSTER BOOKS FOR YOUNG READERS is a trademark
of Simon & Schuster, Inc.
The text for this book is handwritten by Anna Walker.
Manufactured in Singapore
10 9 8 7 6 5 4 3 2 1
CIP data for this book is available from the Library of Congress.
ISBN: 978-1-4169-8317-0

I Love Christmas

by Anna Walker

SIMON & SCHUSTER BOOKS FOR YOUNG READERS
New York • London • Toronto • Sydney

My name is Ollie.

I love Christmas.

I love crinkly paper,
tinsel, and string,
my Christmas reindeer
with one little wing.

I love the cow
and happy sheep,

the star, the donkey,
and the baby asleep.

I love to glitter,

stick,

and make,

and help bake Nanna's
Christmas cake.

I love stars in the sky,

and joyful angels

dancing by.

I love to sing about Santa—
he's coming tonight!

I love to watch the twinkly Christmas light.

But what I love best
is to sit on my bed
and listen for Santa's
sleigh bells with Fred.